TESSA POTTER

THE GHOSTS OF GOLFHAWK SCHOOL

Illustrated by Gillian Hunt

WAYLAND

Chapter One

Mrs Peaks said it was hard starting a new school near the end of term and we should all try and make friends with Kirsty Morgan. But I couldn't. She annoyed me right from the start. It was the way she stood there that first morning, wanting everyone to notice her. Her face was white,

her dark black hair wild and tangled. She just stood in the doorway and wouldn't move. Mrs Peaks had to get up from her desk and go over to her.

"What's the matter, Kirsty dear? You're late into class."

Kirsty didn't answer.

"Please come and sit down," said Mrs Peaks.

Kirsty still didn't move. She stared at Mrs Peaks, her eyes strange and wide. Then at last she spoke. "There's a body in the boys' cloakroom, miss," she whispered.

Tom Wilson snorted and Emma giggled but the rest of us sat quietly.

"I'm sorry, dear, I didn't quite catch that," said Mrs Peaks.

"She says there's a body in the boys' cloakroom," squealed Emma.

"What were you doing in the boys' cloakroom?" asked Mrs Peaks.

"I couldn't find where to put my coat," said Kirsty quietly. "I got lost."

"Well, come into class now, please."

"There is something there," she insisted.

Then my friend Martin nudged me and put up his hand. "Shall Dan and I go and  check it out, Mrs Peaks?"

I glared at Martin. I didn't want to get involved.

"Thank you, Martin, that would be helpful. Somebody's probably dropped their coat. It is quite gloomy in there. Now please sit down, Kirsty."

Kirsty walked slowly to her place. She stared at Mrs Peaks again, shaking her head. "It wasn't a coat."

"Off you go, Martin and Dan," said Mrs Peaks briskly. "Be as quick as you can."

Chapter Two

When we were outside the classroom I grabbed Martin's arm. "What did you do that for?"

Martin just grinned, "Come on!"

The cloakrooms were at the end of the long dark corridor. A musty smell of damp and disinfectant drifted towards us.

Golfhawk School was old and crumbling. It would have made a good set for a horror film with its winding corridors and high towering ceilings. It was all right when lots of people were around, but it wasn't a good place to be alone in. And that was even before Kirsty arrived and began pretending to see things.

Anyway making up horror and ghost stories was something Martin and I did, it was our thing. We used to scare the infants until Miss Wade the headteacher found out. Some of the little ones wouldn't go to the toilet on their own because of the stories we'd made up about the cloakrooms. We got really told off for it.

"Do you think she did see something?" asked Martin as we hurried along the dim corridor.

"Don't be silly," I said. "We know there's nothing really there. It'll just be a pile of clothes like Mrs Peaks said."

We reached the door at last. I opened it slowly.

"You first," said Martin, pushing me from behind.

It was dark in there. The only window was high up near the ceiling. My hand groped for the light switch.

The light above us whirred and flickered for a second, then nothing.

"The light's gone," I groaned.

Slowly our eyes grew used to the gloom and we moved forward. Coats hung hunched around the room like headless phantoms.

"Let's go back," whispered Martin.

"No wait. This was your idea. What's that?" I said catching sight of a huddled shape on the floor below the window. "Over there, that's what she must have seen."

"There's a foot sticking out..." began Martin.

"It's probably just a trainer," I said.

But as I bent down, I felt strange. I shuddered, my head began to reel.

Suddenly the door slammed shut behind us.

Chapter Three

We turned and ran screaming towards the door. We tore it open.

Miss Wade was standing in the corridor, glaring at us.

"What on earth are you two doing in here in the dark?"

She switched on the light.

"It was broken, miss," I stammered. "Mrs Peaks sent us."

Miss Wade frowned. "I thought I'd warned you that this changing room nonsense had to stop. Get back to class. I'll speak to Mrs Peaks later."

She glanced at the pile of clothes. We could now clearly see some coats and shoe bags, heaped up in a way that did look as though someone was lying there.

"You can put those away during your next break," Miss Wade told us.

Back in class we told Mrs Peaks what had happened. "There wasn't a body. It was just a pile of clothes," said Martin. "And Miss Wade is making us clear them up!"

Mrs Peaks turned to Kirsty. "There you are, dear. There's nothing to worry about. It seems some of the boys haven't been putting away their things. Now let's all get on with our work."

"I bet she did it," I whispered to Martin. "I bet she put those things on the floor herself."

There wasn't much of dinner play left by the time Martin and I had finished tidying up. When we got outside there was a whole gang round Kirsty.

"As soon as I got here, I knew it was one of those places," she was saying.

"What places?" asked Josie.

"You know, where things aren't quite right. Places too near the edge."

"She means ghosts," I butted in, "and there's no such thing."

"And we thought you were the spooky one, Dan," laughed Josie.

Kirsty turned to me. "I'm sorry you had to clear up because of me, but I did see something. There was a little boy there. He was lying on his side."

I pulled Martin's arm. "Come on, this is boring."

We ran off to the other side of the playground. I glanced towards Kirsty as the bell went. She was pointing to the middle of the playground.

"What's she been going on about now?" I whispered to Josie as we lined up.

"Something about a cold spot which no one ever walks over," said Josie.

Chapter Four

Of course there were cold places in the playground which everyone avoided, like between the kitchens and infants' building. The wind really whistled through there.

But I didn't believe Kirsty's thing about cold spots.

It was last break and everyone had gathered round her again. "Look to the right of that tree," she was saying. "No one ever

walks over that part of the playground. See those girls with a football, they'll swerve round it, even if the ball goes that way."

"Mrs Peaks is going towards it now!" shrieked Josie.

"She won't cross it, she'll change direction. There!" cried Kirsty, triumphantly as Mrs Peaks swerved for no reason.

"It's rubbish, just coincidence," I said.

"OK, why don't you stand there if it's just rubbish?" grinned Josie.

"Yes, go on," shouted several voices.

"Dan's scared," giggled Tom.

I glared at him. "Don't be stupid." I said, hating Kirsty now. She'd started all this.

I began to walk slowly towards the place Kirsty had pointed to, although it was hard to work out exactly where the spot was

supposed to be. I turned to look back at the others. They were cheering me on, all except Kirsty. She was standing very quietly staring straight ahead. I walked on a little further…

I don't really remember exactly what happened next. I felt suddenly sick and very shivery. My legs felt heavy but I forced myself to keep walking. I closed my eyes.

My head began to swim. Then everything

went quiet. There was no noise at all in the playground. Just a terrible crushing silence. I thought my head was going to burst.

A moment later Martin was beside me. He sounded anxious. "Are you all right, Dan? What happened? You look awful."

I shook him off. "Of course I'm all right. I just felt sick. It was those burgers at dinner."

Then Josie was there too. "Are you OK? Do you believe Kirsty now?"

I glared at her. "Nothing happened."

Mrs Peaks came over and took me inside and said she hoped I wasn't getting flu. She let me sit quietly until home time. I felt terrible. I wished Kirsty Morgan hadn't come to our school. Everything had been all right until she came.

Chapter Five

Things were even worse when I got to school the next day. I found that Martin was off sick and Mrs Peaks was ill too. Then I got put next to Kirsty Morgan in assembly.

When I tried to move, Miss Wade told me off and made me stand out at the side. I could see Kirsty's face clearly from here. She wasn't joining in the singing at all. She looked strange and pale. She kept staring at the stage behind Miss Wade.

Then she began to sway. I thought she was going to fall but the next moment the hymn was over and everyone was filing out.

Back in the classroom Josie had her arm round Kirsty. "What's the matter? Did you see something?" But Kirsty wouldn't say anything.

Then Miss Wade marched in. "It seems we have a bit of a flu epidemic on our hands," she said. "Fortunately we have a student teacher in school today and he will be taking you this morning."

As Miss Wade began to do the register, an awful thought came to me. Suppose she asked me to take it back. It was always me she seemed to notice. I sunk lower into my seat. Suddenly I couldn't bear the thought of

crossing the hall alone. Not after the look on Kirsty's face in assembly.

At this time of the morning the hall was completely deserted. Mrs Peaks always let us take the register back in pairs. The huge room echoed with your footsteps.

The faded curtains on the stage moved sometimes, as though someone or something was lurking there. And sometimes you could hear a soft crying sound, like the wind moaning...

I heard the register snap shut and Miss Wade's voice booming. "Daniel, stop slouching! Take the register to the office, please."

I stood up, my heart pounding. "Can someone else come as well?" I stammered. "Mrs Peaks usually sends two of us…"

Miss Wade laughed, "It hardly takes two to carry a register, Daniel."

I heard Tom Wilson snigger.

I caught sight of Kirsty staring at me. Her anxious look made me feel even worse. I took the register and began to walk slowly towards the door.

Chapter Six

The door opened just as I reached it.

"Excuse me, is this Year Six?" asked a red-faced young man.

Miss Wade got up from her desk. "Come in, Mr Hicks." She took the register from me.

Relieved, I slipped back to my seat.

When Miss Wade had gone, Mr Hicks began to hand out some maps.

"We are going to begin a local history project this morning. Do any of you know how old Golfhawk School is?"

Josie's hand shot up. "About a hundred years, sir. When we were in the infants, we all had to dress up."

Mr Hicks nodded. "The school was founded in the 1890s." He paused.

"However, this 1830 map shows that there was already a small building here long before then. The new school was built around this building, so parts of your school are actually much older than a hundred years…"

"Oooh, spooky," shouted Tom Wilson.

Mr Hicks frowned at Tom, but continued. "The old building was once an orphanage.

It was closed down after all the orphans died
in a terrible cholera epidemic which swept
through the town. So many people died
there was no room left in the churchyard
and the rest of the dead had to be buried
elsewhere in huge pits. The poor orphan
children were buried together in just such
an unmarked grave and forgotten. This
epidemic led to many changes and
improvements in the town..."

34

Mr Hick's speech was suddenly interrupted by a terrible moaning sound. It was coming from Kirsty. She was rolling her head from side to side. Then she went limp and slumped down on to her desk.

"She's fainted," screamed Josie.

Mr Hicks looked worried. "Fetch Miss Wade," he shouted.

"Perhaps she's dead," said Emma.

Miss Wade arrived. She clapped her hands briskly. "Everyone back in their seats, please."

Kirsty lifted her head. Her eyes were wild. "I saw them in the hall," she sobbed, "the little children…"

"Kirsty Morgan thinks the school's haunted miss," said Josie. "She keeps seeing things. Mr Hicks said a lot of children died here once – there was an epidemic, like now."

"And people got put into pits," said Tom.

"I feel sick," wailed Sarah.

"And me, miss," someone else cried.

"Are we all going to die?" wailed Sam.

"Stop all this nonsense now!" shouted Miss Wade. "We have a forty-eight-hour tummy bug in the school, not cholera! And there are no ghosts here!" she said, glaring at me.

She led Kirsty from the room. "And if any of you feel ill tomorrow, please stay at home." She turned grimly to the student teacher, "I suggest you explore a more suitable topic, Mr Hicks."

Chapter Seven

The next day Martin and Mrs Peaks were
still away. But Kirsty was there. She seemed
to have got over her 'flu' really quickly.
Miss Wade was taking us again, but I was
due to help in Miss Soper's reception class.
Some of us helped with Miss Soper's nativity
play every year. It was the dress rehearsal
that afternoon.

That morning we were helping the angels
finish the wings for their costumes. The
wings were made of wire and card with shiny
paper and tinsel stuck on. The infants did
the sticking and we had to sew the wings on
to long white robes made from sheets.
My infant got loads of glue everywhere.

I was sorry when I had to go back into class. Everywhere was quiet, as though a dark cloud had fallen. The whole place felt different, strange and shivery. It was the same all afternoon. No one joked or laughed. There was no more upset from Kirsty, but she looked so ill and pale, Miss Wade said she should have stayed at home.

After school she came over to me and
Josie. I wondered what she was going to go
on about this time. "I saw them again," she
whispered, "the little children. They were
standing in the playground in long white
robes. They'd risen up from the ground,
from the dark pit..."

I nearly laughed out loud with relief. I realized then that Kirsty really had just been making it all up. Not so much making things up, as getting things wrong, getting carried away and exaggerating.

"Those weren't ghosts, silly! They were Miss Soper's angels!" I told her. "You must have seen the infants coming back from their dress rehearsal."

Josie put her arm round Kirsty. "Come on, I'll walk home with you," she said. I felt almost light-headed as I watched them walk away. There wasn't anything strange about the school at all. Kirsty had just imagined it.

I set off for home myself. I was nearly there when I realized I'd left my bag behind. Miss Wade had set us some work – she'd kill me if it wasn't done. It wasn't quite dark yet. If I hurried there might still be some teachers around. I turned and began to run.

I was out of breath by the time I reached
school. It was very cold now and I was
shivering. A thin mist was beginning to come
down. There were no lights on anywhere,
but the gates were still open. I walked slowly
into the playground.

I saw them straight away – Miss Soper's
angels, a whole group of them. I couldn't
understand what they were still doing there.
Why had Miss Soper kept them back so late?
Was there another rehearsal? And what were
they doing with no shoes on? It was freezing.

Then as I stared at their long white robes, the truth slowly dawned. I felt the blood drain from my face. Kirsty Morgan had been right all along. As I watched those sad tiny figures, I knew. These weren't Miss Soper's angels at all. These angels had no wings...

If you have enjoyed this book, why not try these other creepy titles:

The Claygate Hound by Jan Dean
It's the school trip to Claygate, and Zeb and Ryan are ready to explore, until they hear stories about the ghost in the woods. It all sounds like a stupid story. But then the boys start to see shadows moving in the trees and eyes glistening in the darkness. Could the Claygate Hound really exist?

Beware the Wicked Web by Anthony Masters
Where had the enormous, dusty spider's web come from? The sticky, silky folds had filled the attic room, and were now clinging to Rob and Sam as they explored the room. In the centre of the web was a huge egg, which was just about to hatch…

Danny and the Sea of Darkness by David Clayton
When does a dream become reality? Danny wakes one night to find himself out at sea during a terrible storm. As he falls overboard into the icy water Danny wonders if he will ever return from the Sea of Darkness.

Time Flies by Mary Hooper
The large oak box looked like the perfect place to hide, but Lucy could never have imagined what powers lay inside. Lucy steps back in time to a strange and scary world. Can she find her way home again before it's too late?

Ghost on the Landing by Eleanor Allen
Jack wakes in the night screaming in fear. His sister's ghost stories about Aunt Stella's spooky old house must have been giving him nightmares. But was it just a bad dream or does the ghost on the landing really exist?